Delilah
Alone

Also by Jenny Nimmo

Delilah and the Dogspell
Delilah and the Dishwasher Dogs
Hot Dog, Cool Cat
Seth and the Strangers
Ill Will, Well Nell
Tatty Apple

For older readers
Milo's Wolves
The Rinaldi Ring
Ultramarine
Griffin's Castle

The Snow Spider trilogy
The Snow Spider
Emlyn's Moon
The Chestnut Soldier

Jenny Nimmo

Delilah
Alone

Illustrated by
Georgien Overwater

mammoth

For Lynda Edwards

First published in Great Britain 1997
by Mammoth
Reissued 2001 by Mammoth
an imprint of Egmont Children's Books Limited
a division of Egmont Holding Limited
239 Kensington High Street, London, W8 6SA

Text copyright © 1997 Jenny Nimmo
Illustrations copyright © 1997 Georgien Overwater
Cover illustration copyright © 2001 Chris Priestley

The moral rights of the author, illustrator and cover illustrator have been asserted

ISBN 0 7497 4560 6

10 9 8 7 6 5 4 3 2

A CIP catalogue record for this title is available from the British Library

Printed and bound in Great Britain
by Cox & Wyman Ltd, Reading, Berkshire

Contents

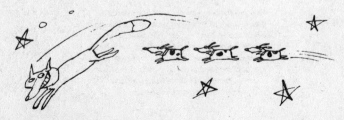

1

The Stranger

'You'd better watch it!'

There was a strange cat sitting on Delilah's wall, in *her* patch of sunshine. None of the neighbourhood cats would have dared to trespass like that. Delilah glared at the stranger, her eyes flashed an angry gold, her wild grey fur fluffed menacingly. She wanted to hiss him away, but she was curious.

'Can't you read the signs?' said the cat. He was the ugliest creature Delilah had ever seen. Dingy colours swirled in his coarse fur like a bowl of stew. A mongrel if ever there was one. Delilah was descended from the household cats of the legendary Queen of Sheba. She had been gifted with strange powers. With one look she could shrink a dog; she could even make them disappear. So why did this miserable looking creature give her the shivers?

'What signs?' she hissed.

'They've just hoovered out the car, haven't they?'

'If you mean *my* Pughs,' Delilah said possessively. 'What of it?'

'They're going on holiday,' declared the stew-cat.

'Of course! It's summer. We always go to a seaside cottage,' retorted Delilah.

'Ho! Ho! Not this year,' said the unpleasant stranger.

Delilah's whiskers bristled. She felt as though a freezing paw had been placed on her neck. How did this awful interloper know the Pughs' plans?

'They're going somewhere hot. Didn't you see the sun-hat Mrs Pugh brought home the

other day? Not to mention the strapless dresses she's been hanging on the line. They're off to France or Spain, I shouldn't wonder. They won't take *you* with them!'

A low growl escaped Delilah. Of course the Pughs would take her. They only went on holiday to give her a break from the noise of traffic and the local riff-raff. It was *her* holiday. She turned her back on the stranger and went indoors. Her family was arguing in the kitchen. This wasn't unusual. Delilah sat outside the door and tried to make out what was going on.

The strange cat had guessed right. The Pughs were going to France so they couldn't take Delilah with them because of the quarantine laws.

'How about a cattery?' Mr Pugh had just suggested.

Edward was appalled. 'A cattery? How could you, Dad?' he cried. 'Delilah's special. Only ordinary cats go there.'

'We could take her to Auntie Betty's,' said Mrs Pugh. 'She's got ever such a nice garden.'

'Auntie Betty's got a dog!' wailed Edward. 'How d'you think Delilah would feel with a great big dog sniffing round her all day?'

'I've no idea,' admitted Mrs Pugh, who was secretly afraid of Delilah. She would have been very happy to sell her to the pet shop, if only Edward hadn't been so ridiculously fond of her.

Edward had a flash of inspiration. 'I'm going to see Annie next door. We'll sort something out. I'm *not* having Delilah shunted off to strangers. She'll never speak to me again.' Leaping out of the kitchen, Edward almost tripped over Delilah, who couldn't restrain a snarl of disapproval. She hated it when Edward was clumsy.

'Don't worry, Delilah,' Edward said. 'You won't go to a cattery, I promise you! Come and see Annie with me.'

'That cat never speaks to anyone anyway,'

Mr Pugh mumbled when Edward had gone.

'Except to demand food,' Mrs Pugh reminded him, 'or a clean blanket.'

Annie Watkin was grooming an exceptionally fine black cat, when Edward came bounding into her garden. Tudor had been a very nervous

kitten, but fostered by Delilah, he had grown into a bit of a hero. Delilah was rather proud of him.

'Help me, Annie!' Edward begged. 'We're going to France and I can't take Delilah. Will you look after her for me?'

'Course,' said Annie. 'But Mum won't let her sleep in the house.'

'She won't have to. She can stay in our house. Just leave her meals in the porch twice a day,

11

with two handfuls of Biscats at bedtime. She can use her cat-flap to come and go whenever she likes.'

'I suppose she only eats expensive stuff,' said Annie.

'Well, yes,' Edward admitted. 'But I'll bring you a month's supply before we leave. Just in case she's extra hungry. Annie you're brilliant. I'll buy you a present.'

'It's a deal,' said Annie.

Delilah and Tudor exchanged glances. What was going on?

The Pughs were up very early on Saturday morning. Delilah prowled round the house, cross and bewildered. The cases were carried out to the car, but not her basket. Her family breezed through the rooms, gathering up possessions, shouting at each other hysterically. And then Edward was hugging the breath out of her, and murmuring 'good-bye' with tears in his eyes.

Delilah followed her family down the garden path. She watched them climb into the car, expecting Edward to bend down and help her in. But he didn't. They closed all the doors and left her on the pavement. And then the white car sped down the road, while Edward, waving

from the rear window, grew smaller and
smaller and smaller.

And then they were gone.

'I told you so,' said a smug voice from the
wall.

2

Abandoned

Delilah couldn't really believe it. She called Edward's name over and over again. Her desperate wails woke the neighbourhood and sent the birds into a terrible twitter.

'What a din!' cried Annie, throwing open her window. She saw Delilah sitting by the Pughs' front gate and decided to cheer her up with an early breakfast.

Tudor followed Annie into the Pughs' garden. Delilah rushed up to him bleating, 'They've gone. Can you believe it? I've been abandoned. Me, of all cats! Edward has gone on holiday without me!'

Tudor had never seen Delilah looking so agitated. 'They wouldn't leave you for more than a day,' he told her. 'They'll be back tonight.'

'If you believe that, you'll believe anything,' remarked the scruffy looking monster that slipped out of the Pughs' flower-bed.

'Where did he come from?' murmured Annie as she spooned two generous helpings of Top-Cat into the bowl beside Delilah's cat-flap.

'Buzz off, you!' Tudor hissed at the stranger.

'Mr Fudge, if you please,' said the cat. 'You might as well get used to my name. I'm coming to live here.'

'Over my dead body,' snarled Delilah and she flew at him with an ear-splitting shriek. Tudor joined in and they chased the monster over the fence and into the fields at the back of the house. Mr Fudge couldn't be caught but Delilah and

Tudor didn't give up until they were sure they had driven the intruder off their territory. 'He won't be back,' Tudor assured Delilah.

Delilah wasn't so sure. There was something evil about Mr Fudge. It pricked her to her very bones. She had never smelt a cat so full of spite, so downright mean. She felt better for the exercise, however, and Tudor had cheered her up with his comforting conviction that the Pughs would be back before dark. They parted at Delilah's gate and went off for a well-deserved nap.

Both cats dozed all day. At tea-time Annie dutifully filled Delilah's bowls, one with Top-Cat and one with milk. She noticed that the strange cat was sitting on Delilah's wall again and made a shooing noise at it. The cat hissed back. It was a wicked-looking animal. Annie wasn't going to argue. Besides, a wind had sprung up and she wanted to try out her new kite.

Annie took her kite to the highest point in the field. She began to let out the string as she ran down the hill. The kite sailed behind her, higher and higher, a great blue and yellow bird. Too late, Annie saw the tree. She tried to draw the kite out of its way, but it caught the string and the blue and yellow bird flopped helplessly into the leaves. 'Bother!' Annie groaned.

The tree was a broad oak with a great many thick branches. It looked easy to climb. Annie ran at the tree, clutched the lower branches and hauled herself up. She was just about to place her foot on a sturdy branch, when curiosity got the better of her and she became interested in a

fight that was going on between two boys in a garden at the end of her road. Distracted by the fight, Annie put all her weight on a flimsy twig, instead of the branch. The twig snapped and down went Annie. 'Oooooooooh!' she screamed as she tumbled into a painful heap.

Luckily Mrs Watkin heard her through the

kitchen window. She found her daughter groaning beside the tree. Her kite was still dangling several feet above her.

'My leg! My leg!' moaned Annie. 'Ooooh! I think it's broken.'

It was.

Annie was rushed to hospital. She would have to stay there overnight.

Meanwhile Mr Fudge had found Delilah's bowls. He wolfed down the Top-Cat. 'Delicious,' he murmured, licking his lips, and then he lapped up every drop of milk. 'Divine,' he purred, and went back to sit on Delilah's wall. After a good wash, he tucked in his paws, curled his tail round his body and closed his eyes. But he didn't sleep. Mr Fudge was making plans for a rosy future.

When Delilah found both her bowls empty at tea-time she was annoyed, but not angry. Edward would give her an extra helping later, she decided. She went back into the house and inspected the kitchen. All the cupboards were firmly closed, the rubbish bin was empty. No crumbs on the floor. No smells in the sink. It was unusual. Eerie. Delilah eyed the fridge. She had learned how to open it but knew it was forbidden. However, these were exceptional circumstances. Delilah leapt for the handle. The door swung open. The fridge was empty!

Delilah felt faint. She went to her basket and curled up, shivering with shock. Something awful had happened. Perhaps the Pughs had left forever! Delilah didn't want to live alone.

Night fell but Edward didn't come home. Delilah climbed out of her basket and went to visit Tudor. 'They haven't come back,' she told him bitterly. 'They've abandoned me.'

Tudor couldn't believe this. 'They wouldn't go without making arrangements for you,' he said.

'I haven't had tea,' Delilah growled, 'and the fridge is empty.'

This was extraordinary. Tudor had always considered his foster-mother to be a rather pampered cat. Her food was superior, her basket regularly hoovered, her velvet cushions cleaned. She had a silver-backed fur-brush, an exercise machine and vitamin pills twice a week. Something strange was going on. And what had happened to Annie?

'Annie's missing too,' he told Delilah.

'And have you gone without supper?'

Tudor had to admit that Mrs Watkin had provided him with a fairly adequate meal, but she wasn't quite herself. Perhaps Delilah and he were having a sort of nightmare. 'It'll be better tomorrow,' he said cheerfully.

'Huh!' muttered Delilah. She marched back to the Pughs' garden with Tudor following. Suddenly she stopped, with one paw raised and her tail as stiff as a broomstick.

Mr Fudge was sitting on the wall again. He was staring at Delilah, his eyes bright with victory, and his body swaying with silent laughter.

That did it. 'I'm going,' growled Delilah.

'Where?' gasped Tudor.

'Anywhere,' she said, and turning her back on Mr Fudge she ran into the back garden. 'Good-bye!' she called as she leapt to the top of the fence. For a moment she hesitated and then, gazing back at Tudor she said, 'You've been a good son, Tudor, I'm proud of you, and I'll miss you.'

'Good-bye!' mewed Tudor. Still, he did nothing. He was too dazed by the awful turn of events. As he watched the great tail disappear over the fence he was overcome by a terrible foreboding. Would he ever see Delilah again?

3

Delilah's Journey

Anger kept Delilah going. She wanted to put as great a distance as possible between herself and Mr Fudge. Whenever she stopped to rest she remembered Edward and what he had done to her, and it made her run faster. By midnight, Delilah was miles from home. Lost. The only light came from the moon. There were no human sounds at all, only the wind sighing across the grass. Delilah crept into a bed of dry bracken and slept. A curlew woke her, crying over her head. She thought it was calling her name, and then she opened her eyes and remembered everything. She stood up, shook her great blanket of fur, and stepped out into the dawn.

Delilah wondered if she was on top of the world. She stood in a great field, without fences, that stretched as far as the horizon. It was covered with short tough grass, bracken and flowers. And it was alive with animals. Larks sang, curlews called, buzzards swooped and hovered, rabbits hopped, sheep grazed and mice and voles scurried in the undergrowth. There was enough food to last Delilah forever. She set about catching breakfast.

When she had eaten her fill of mice, she set off towards a distant range of hills. The sun was just beginning to rise, the air was warm and food plentiful. Delilah decided to put aside all dark thoughts of Edward and his betrayal. She would enjoy herself.

She travelled slowly now, stopping for snacks whenever she felt like it. She found a sheep track that was easy on the paws and found herself descending into a wooded valley. It was here that she heard the sounds that she most feared. Barking and howling.

Delilah stopped dead. Where could she hide? The howling was fast approaching. A fox shot out of the trees and rushed past her, its yellow eyes starting with fear. The scent of terror that the fox left on the air made Delilah dizzy. She ran to the nearest tree and clawed her way up

the rough bark. A second later a pack of hounds burst into view and surrounded the tree. The fox had left his scent in a hollow where the thick roots twisted round the base of the tree. The pack had their noses to the ground and then their leader spied Delilah. He began to bark. Thirty dog muzzles were raised and filled the air with howling. Delilah's heart pounded. She knew what she had to do, but it was a long time since she had used a dogspell.

She closed her eyes, deafened herself to every sound and concentrated. Below her the thirty hounds began to whimper as they saw a creature with glittering fur, and whiskers blue with electricity. Unable to move they gazed at the shower of colourful sparks that fell on their noses, on their backs and tails, and on their ears and eyelids. And in horror they watched each other shrink and fade, droop, shrivel and melt until every dog was the size of a mouse. And then they ran away – squeaking.

A few moments later, the huntsmen appeared on tall chestnut horses. They scratched their heads under their black velvet hats and muttered in bewildered and grumbling voices. The woods and fields were empty and the whole world eerily silent. Had their precious hounds completely vanished?

If the riders had searched beneath their horses, they would have seen their hounds scampering about, trying to adjust to their new life as midget creatures. But it is doubtful

whether the huntsmen would have believed their eyes. They went home angry and mystified. And several days later their story was printed in the local paper under the heading, 'Mysterious Disappearance of the Brynholm Pack.'

Delilah always liked a good wash after a spell, because the sparks left her fur rather stiff and uncomfortable. Just as she was getting to grips with a hind leg, the fox trotted out of his hiding place. 'How did you do that?' he asked, gazing up at her in breathless admiration.

'It's just something I can do, when the occasion warrants it.'

'Amazing,' sighed the fox. He watched a tiny dog scuttle across his foot but couldn't bring himself to do anything about it. 'D'you think I could learn?' he asked.

'Not a chance,' said Delilah. 'It's a gift bestowed on me by Mustapha Marzavan, the magician, when I was born. I'm afraid it's only for cats, not foxes.'

'Pity,' said the fox. 'But thanks for saving my life.'

'You're welcome,' Delilah said graciously, unwilling to admit that her only thought had been for herself.

The fox loped off, and for the first time in

many months, Delilah began to think about Mustapha Marzavan and his youngest daughter. They would never have abandoned her. They were the most cat-friendly humans in the world. Somehow she must find them. Her life with Edward was over. She decided to look for a town and after several days of peaceful hunting and sleeping in the fresh, warm air, she found herself beside a wide, roaring motorway, covered in cars on their way to town. Hidden by the scruffy vegetation that grew beside the road, Delilah followed the great beast south.

Just before dawn on a Sunday morning,

Delilah found herself on the edge of a city. The street lights cast an angry glare into the dark sky, but as Delilah plunged deeper into the city, she found herself in a narrow street, filled with inky shadows, and something else – a smell that took her back to the days she had spent as a kitten, caged in a boat on the wild salty sea.

Delilah had never felt so alone. Outside a grim, derelict building she sat down and howled out her despair. And to her great surprise there came an answer. It was a smothered, melancholy sound but Delilah knew that another cat was calling her name.

4

Escape

'Am I dreaming?' Delilah wondered aloud. 'Who knows me in a place so far from home?' She looked up and searched the dark windows for a movement, for any sign that something lived beyond the grimy panes. The voice went on.

When she saw the cat at last, her heart nearly stopped beating, for it was herself she saw, or rather, a dismal and pathetic copy. Delilah walked uncertainly towards the narrow window. The other cat pressed its face closer to the glass and called Delilah's name again. For a moment the two cats eyed each other, and then the other cat spoke again, 'Don't you remember me?'

And now Delilah recognized the poor creature. They hadn't seen each other since kittenhood but Delilah had no doubt that she was looking at her dear sister Sorayah.

'Sorayah, what has happened to you?' she cried.

'It's a long story,' Sorayah said, 'and I may not live to tell it.'

'Why?' gasped Delilah.

'No one wants me.' Sorayah's eyes were a dim, filmy gold. 'Tomorrow they're going to put me down. Destroy me. It's happened to all the others that were brought here.'

'I won't let them! I'm going to get you out.'

'Impossible,' whimpered her sister.

A window opened further down the street, and a human voice shouted, 'Shut up, or I'll shoot you!'

Delilah growled softly. She scanned the building for a way in and saw a small window,

29

with the top section very slightly open. Beneath the window there was a mound of black rubbish bags. Delilah ran at the black mountain and scrambled to the top. Teetering on the slippery summit she leapt for the tiny opening. Now she was balanced on a thin iron frame, with her head against the top pane. She crouched under the glass and dropped into a small room. A lavatory, and the door was open. So far so good. She could still hear Sorayah calling, and followed the sound, getting closer and closer. She entered a dank, evil-smelling room, with cages piled to the ceiling on every side. Some of the cages were empty, but others were filled with silent birds, or small dejected creatures: gerbils, hamsters, mice, rabbits and even a bleary-eyed puppy too ill to worry her.

Delilah was horrified. 'Oh, Sorayah,' she groaned, 'where are you?'

'Here,' came a voice from the end of the room.

Sorayah was boxed into the window by a stout wooden door, and the door was bolted both at the top and the bottom. Delilah climbed over a crate of rabbits, stood on her back legs and thrust a paw at the top bolt. It was stiff with rust. She swiped at it again. She leapt up and bit at it. The bolt moved. Delilah raised both paws and pushed with all her strength. I can do it, she told herself, with a magician's help. The bolt slid open. The lower bolt was easy. The big cat stepped back as the door swung open.

'Sorayah!'

'Delilah!'

The two grey cats brushed cheeks and licked each other welcome. They murmured softly and then Delilah said, 'Tell me! Tell me! Tell it all!'

'First let us get out of here,' said Sorayah. 'It's such a terrible place.'

'Terrible,' agreed Delilah, springing from the rabbits' crate. 'But first, we must free all these creatures. They don't deserve to die in this way.'

'Then let us do it quickly, sister. They always come by first light, the murderers.'

The two cats set about opening cages. They used their teeth, their noses, their paws and claws, and even their hard grey heads. They bit and pushed, hooked and pulled, and although Sorayah was very weak, she did her best. Soon every catch and bolt, every lid and door had been opened, and as the dawn spilled through the window, the room began to fill with feebly fluttering birds, and bewildered scrawny creatures. The cats' hunting instincts were completely overcome by pity.

'Oh, hurry, please! I'm sure they're coming.' As Sorayah spoke they could hear the rumble of an engine.

'Quick! Quick! Quick!' she screamed.

Delilah saw a large cracked pane in a window close to Sorayah's prison, and jumped on to a box a few feet from the sill. 'Be brave,' she commanded, 'and follow me!'

Terrified creatures watched the great grey cat

fly at the glass. Squeaks of amazement broke out as the broken pane fell and shattered in the street.

'Hurry!' called Delilah. Her thick coat had protected her from the broken glass, but splinters still hung on her fur like tiny diamonds.

Sorayah dropped down beside her sister, followed by the birds. The narrow street resounded with the rustle of beating wings and the whistling of high, anxious voices. Timid rabbits emerged from their cages, sniffing the air suspiciously.

'No time to lose!' called the cats. 'Jump! Now!'

So the rabbits jumped, amid a scuttling scramble of smaller creatures that leapt, dropped, slithered and fell onto the cobbles.

The approaching van increased its speed, and Delilah could see the driver. He was a thick-set man with a broad red face and he wore a black jacket. A crowd of frantic birds flew across the windscreen and the van screeched to a halt. The driver jumped out and waved the birds aside, brushing his wide arms in the air like the blades of a windmill. And then, ignoring the smaller creatures spinning round his feet, he rushed at Delilah.

'I'll have you!' he roared.

As the cats sped away from him, Delilah could hear Sorayah's painful breathing. She knew her poor sister didn't have the strength to run far. 'Keep close to me,' Delilah whispered, 'and we'll find somewhere to hide.'

But there seemed to be no hiding place. The long street began to fill with light, as the thunder of heavy boots drew closer.

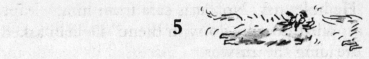

5

Sorayah's Story

When the two cats reached the end of the street, Delilah searched vainly in the maze of roads that confronted her until she saw a large blue truck, just a few feet away. 'Under here,' Delilah hissed, and bolted under it.

Sorayah crept in beside her. Peering from the shadows, the cats could see two heavy boots arrive on the pavement in front of them. The boots stomped about, kicking the ground, while their owner swore lustily in all directions.

Delilah moved closer to her sister and crouched motionless against Sorayah's trembling body. 'Sssh!' she whispered, so softly a mouse wouldn't have heard her.

They stayed in this position for several minutes, while the boots crashed up and down. At last the man marched back into the alley where he'd left his truck. Sorayah laid her head on her paws, faint with exhaustion. 'He would have taken you, that dreadful man,' she said. 'He has a net. No cat is safe from him.'

'What does he do with them?' Delilah asked, dreading the answer.

'If their fur is smooth, it is taken to line human coats. Fluffy cats, like us, are popular with children, so we survive if we are good-natured. Others, whose fur has deteriorated, are . . .' Sorayah was too distressed to continue.

'I can guess,' Delilah said gently, aware that her sister fell into the third category. Experiments, she thought grimly, and not for the first time did she long for the power to shrink humans. If only she could have shrivelled that horrible man.

'We must go to our brothers,' Sorayah said. 'They'll know what to do.'

'Isam and Casimir? They're here, in this city?' Delilah was astonished.

'They escaped, I'll tell you everything. Oh, Delilah, I feel so much more hopeful now that you have found me.'

Three years ago, when the four of them were kittens, they had been sitting in the pet

department of a very famous store. And then Delilah had been lifted out of their enclosure. Sorayah was terrified. She couldn't imagine what had happened. An elderly woman had gazed in at Sorayah and her brothers, and before they knew what was happening, they were all three put in a box together. There followed a terrifying journey in the dark, but in the morning the three kittens found themselves on a warm rug before a blazing fire.

'We led a delightful life,' said Sorayah. 'We wanted for nothing. We had soft cushions, a garden full of fragrance, toys, fine food and oh, so much love. And then, one morning a few weeks ago, when we went to greet our dear friend, we found that she wouldn't wake up.'

'Dead, most probably,' said Delilah. 'It happens.'

Sorayah shuddered at this remark and continued rather shakily, 'They carried her away and while we were still loud with our grief, they took us from our fine house, and that – that man got hold of us.

'At first we stayed in his shop in the city, but I couldn't eat the food he gave me. I was so ill. I begged my brothers to escape while they could. They didn't want to go without me but I knew it would be impossible for them to gnaw through the bars of my cage without being caught. So I pretended to be dead. Next morning the man took me to that dreadful place where you found me. I think this would have been my last day. We were all doomed. We knew it.'

'But you are alive, sister,' Delilah told her firmly. 'Soon your fur will be thick and your eyes bright. Now, tell me, where can we find our brothers?'

'Well, it's only a rumour, but I heard they were living close to the sea,' Sorayah said. 'They have become quite famous, you know.'

'Famous. For what?'

'They are champions of the poor,' Sorayah said proudly. 'They steal for the weak and defend the oppressed. They even give lessons in self-defence to stray kittens and other – unfortunates. They are quite fearless, even water doesn't daunt them. In fact I have heard that they have saved more than one drowning kitten from the sea.'

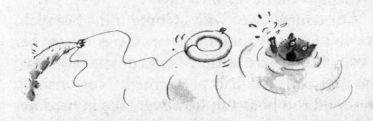

'Well, I can certainly smell the sea. So let's get going before the city wakes up and we're caught in traffic.'

The two cats headed off across a wide road. They walked beneath a building that rose, like a ship, before a sea of strange shrubs; they passed tall blocks of flats with tiny coloured balconies, and walked along a marina where a pretty four-masted schooner rocked on a glittering pool. And then they reached a beach of thick pale sand that stretched down to the water. And the smell of fish reminded Delilah that she was extremely hungry. She thought of all the tiny creatures she could have eaten that morning and, speaking aloud, said, 'No. They were such poor creatures, I couldn't have eaten them.'

'Nor I,' agreed Sorayah. She regarded the deserted beach, looked this way and that and gave a dismal mew. 'Our brothers are not here. There's no hint, no smell, no drifts on the air. Perhaps we'll never find them.'

'Of course we will. Come on, Sorayah, we've a lot of ground to cover.' To entertain her melancholy sister as they walked, she described the dogspells she had performed. Not wishing to sound too boastful, however, she invited her sister to talk about her dogspells.

Sorayah looked embarrassed. 'There haven't been any in my life,' she confessed.

'None? I thought that all our family were gifted.'

'I've led such a sheltered life. There was never any need.'

'Extraordinary,' murmured Delilah.

They now found themselves in the harbour. Fishing boats were moored all along the quay, and, while the city was still asleep, men with crates ran to and fro, their shouts and laughter mingling with the squeal of seabirds. The smell of fish was overpowering.

The two sisters looked into a low building open to the quay. They could see a vast array of shining fish and as they gazed at it hungrily, a huge grey cat with golden eyes bounded out of nowhere. The tail of a gleaming fish hung from his mouth, and close behind him came a dog with a bark like thunder.

'Casimir!' breathed Sorayah. 'He needs help.'

'Watch me, sister,' cried Delilah, 'and you'll remember dogspells!'

6

The Search

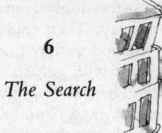

Sorayah ran behind a pile of crates. She was shaking with fright and for a moment couldn't bring herself even to peep at Delilah. But at last a mysterious sound made her curious. She sidled out of her hiding-place and looked for her sister. Delilah had vanished. In the distance the fishermen swung their nets and crates of fish, but just beneath the rumpus Sorayah could detect an eerie undercurrent. It came from a battered-looking shed.

Sorayah crept over to the shed. It was empty. She stepped carefully round to the back, ready to flee at the first sign of danger. But the danger was not for Sorayah. Behind the shed she came upon something so incredible that her pink mouth flew open with a mew of astonishment.

Delilah's coat was an exploding mass of coloured stars, every strand of fur was stiff and glittering, and her whiskers glowed like firesticks. The dog before her was dissolving;

he was evaporating, shrinking. When he was as tiny as a mouse he scuttled away, squeaking with terror.

'Oh!' murmured Sorayah. 'Dogspells are wonderful.'

Dogspells also took a great deal of concentration. Delilah had to go into a sort of trance before she could perform them. Her voice was always a little thin for a few minutes afterwards, so she preferred not to talk. Realizing that Delilah was not quite herself, Sorayah politely gazed at the sky, while her sister washed herself.

'Sorayah,' Delilah said at length. 'I think you should pracise dogspelling.'

'Yes, I can see that it is a very useful accomplishment. But will the dog—er—grow again?'

'Not a chance,' Delilah said smugly. 'Come on, let's find Casimir.'

'He's changed,' said Sorayah. 'He looks so wild and vicious.'

'Changed for the better, then,' said Delilah. 'It isn't safe to be tame when you're out, like we are now, with no home to go to, and no family to take care of you.'

A great sadness clouded Sorayah's golden eyes, and Delilah was struck by the terrible change in her sister. She had been such a happy, spirited kitten; now she was so easily upset, so sad and helpless. She would never survive.

'This won't do at all. You must be more positive, Sorayah.'

'It's been a shock,' explained Sorayah. 'My brothers climbed the wall, often. So they knew. They were prepared. But I was our mistress's favourite, and I never left the garden. Perhaps my brothers didn't want to spoil it for me. I was happy in my ignorance, believing that all humans loved cats and were kind.'

'They should have warned you,' grumbled Delilah. 'It would have been kinder. But now I'm going to find you a meal. With a full belly, life will not seem so bad.'

Sorayah perked up at this and together the sisters made their way along the harbour in search of their brothers. Delilah was tempted to go and beg for a fish, but Sorayah wouldn't hear of it. Her trust in humans had been destroyed forever.

Casimir and Isam had hidden themselves very cleverly. In vain the sisters sniffed the air for a hint of the family scent, but always the smell of fish got in the way. When Sorayah could go no further the two cats crawled in between the thick coils of a pile of rope and curled together, falling fast asleep.

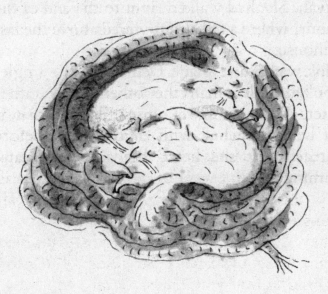

Delilah didn't wake up until it was almost dark. The need for food was now overpowering. Beside her, Sorayah, troubled by nightmares, trembled in her sleep, but it was probably the first sleep she'd had for days so Delilah decided to hunt alone.

The moon was full, the air warm and salty. It was a perfect night for hunting. But as well as food, Delilah hoped to find her brothers. The harbour was now quite silent except for the 'slap-swish' of the sea against the fishing boats. She travelled further than she intended, and it was only when she paused to catch a rat that she realized she couldn't even see where she had left Sorayah. She had walked right to the end of the harbour, where a tall cliff towered above the last warehouse.

This warehouse made Delilah's spine tingle. It looked older than the others, and rather sinister. Delilah's sixth sense told her that it must be approached with caution. But before she reached it she heard the sound of cats, screaming!

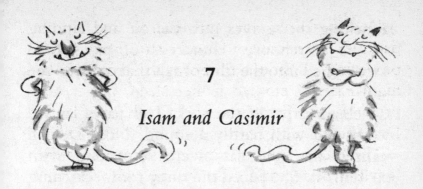

7

Isam and Casimir

Delilah stood still, trying to catch the tone of the screaming cats. Were they crying in pain or in anger? Or were they merely playing? She could detect kitten voices – hundreds of them. What was going on? Her tail bristled. The tall doors were padlocked. Were the kittens prisoners then? Delilah crept round the side of the warehouse. The high windows were all closed and barred. But now she could see that the building backed directly onto the cliff. If she could scramble up the steep, precarious-looking rock, it would be an easy jump onto the roof. Once Delilah began to climb she saw that she was ascending a well-trodden path. Dozens of cats had passed this way. She could smell them and feel the imprint of their paws. She reached a platform of rock, polished smooth by the feet and bodies of many creatures. She could imagine a great crowd of cats, waiting while their companions crouched on the rock before launching themselves into the air and landing on the warehouse. Hundreds of paw-prints were etched into the film of salt that covered the roof.

Delilah leapt off the rock. Her paws landed neatly and with hardly a sound. Now Delilah realized that the cats were screaming with excitement. She paced the rusty roof, searching for a way in. Then she saw it, a gap of a few inches where the thin metal had rusted away altogether. Delilah peered through the hole. Her eyes widened in disbelief as she took in the amazing scene below.

Tall plastic pillars, four or five rows deep, stood all round the interior of the warehouse. Every few yards there was a narrow alley between the pillars. These led to iron ladders fixed to the wall. At the top of the ladders, a balcony ran along each side of the warehouse. Moonlight, slipping through the high windows, illuminated a multi-coloured crowd of cats. They were fighting each other, boxing, biting, clawing, pouncing, gripping and leaping before an audience of kittens and wounded cats, sitting all round the arena. In her wildest dreams Delilah had never imagined such a sight. Where had they all come from? And why were they here? They seemed to be enjoying the fight.

A few feet below the roof, a wide beam ran from wall to wall, directly under the hole. Delilah flattened her stomach, stiffened her tail and dropped through, tail first. Now she was perched on the beam, high above the battling cats and kittens. But directly opposite to her,

and sitting on a similar beam, were two enormous tom cats. They had wild grey fur, huge yellow eyes and whiskers like slim silver spears.

Delilah gasped. 'Isam! Casimir!' she called.

The two toms glared at her. They shouted, in unison, 'Leave, stranger! You haven't been invited.'

At the sound of the fierce voices the other cats stopped fighting and fell silent. All gazed up at the three, almost identical cats.

'It's me, Delilah,' Delilah said as calmly as she could.

'So what?' said one of the toms. Delilah noticed that he had a bent ear.

'So what?' said Delilah huffily. 'You know who Delilah is, I presume. Or have your brains been scrambled?'

'Delilah *who*?' screeched the good-eared tom, smarting from the insult.

'Why, Delilah . . . Delilah . . .' She was about to say Pugh, when she remembered that, of course, her brothers wouldn't know this name.

Slightly flustered, Delilah rearranged herself on the beam.

'I am Delilah Marzavan,' she began quietly, 'daughter of Almira, and I was born somewhere

across the sea, in the great cat parlour of
Mustapha Marzavan, Breeder of Rare Cats. I
was one of a litter of four: Delilah, Sorayah,
Casimir and Isam. And I was the favourite of
Mustapha Marzavan's youngest daughter,
whose name, I confess, I cannot remember.'

The toms were staring at her, immobile on

their beam. 'Have you forgotten?' she asked.

They didn't reply. They arched their backs and paced along their beam in opposite directions, then, leaping simultaneously onto a balcony, they began to approach Delilah.

The cats below watched expectantly, their heads turning first to one tom, then the other. Delilah waited with bowed head. She knew she wouldn't stand a chance if the two huge cats attacked her. She could spring back through the hole in the roof, but they would be upon her before she reached the rock.

She sensed heavy bodies on her beam, heard paws getting closer, smelled a strong male odour. Delilah closed her eyes. 'Don't you know me?' she mewed.

Now they were sniffing her coat, her tail and her ears. 'So!' breathed the good-eared tom at last.

'It is!' added Bent-ear.

'And are you Casimir and Isam?' Delilah asked.

'We are.'

'Casimir,' said the good-eared tom.

'Isam,' said the other.

Delilah wanted to tell them her whole life-history, but she knew that they were not interested in the past just then.

'Why are you here?' she asked.

'We're an army,' replied Casimir, nodding at the cats below, 'or rather we are about to become one. We take fish from the sheds along the quay . . .'

'To feed the unfortunate ones,' said Isam, whose voice was softer than his brother's, 'the homeless ones, the mistreated kittens, the road-wounded and the lost.'

'And we are instructing them in the art of self-defence,' said Casimir proudly. 'We are teaching them that cats are strong, fearless and cunning, higher than other creatures.'

'Noble, wise, worthy of respect,' went on Isam.

'Champions,' added Casimir. 'Emperors of the animal empire.'

'Oh, I agree,' said Delilah, 'whole-heartedly. And I, of course, I can help you.'

'How?' asked Casimir.

'It is possible, brother . . .' began Isam.

'We don't need her,' snorted Casimir. 'Of what use is a pampered well-fed female?'

Delilah was outraged. 'Let me get this straight,' she spat at Casimir. Drawing herself up she faced him squarely, and glaring into eyes as brittle gold as her own, she hissed, 'You pick up strays and kittens, invalids and tramps, and yet you deny your own sister. What sort of a cat are you?'

'An emperor!' yelled Casimir.

'A boastful, puffed-up pig, more like,' screeched Delilah.

Casimir was so surprised he nearly fell off the beam. He couldn't speak, nor could his brother. But before either of them could recover, a great banging resounded through the building. Suddenly the doors were flung open and a flashlight was beamed across the rows of shocked and silent cats.

'What the devil's going on here?' a voice roared. 'Clear out, the lot of you! Go on! SHOO!'

The dazed cats couldn't move.

'Want a bit of encouragement do you? Go on

then, Bruiser, get them!'

A huge blood-hound bounded into the warehouse. It picked up a kitten and shook it like a rag. The other cats squealed in horror but could do nothing.

'Fight!' howled Casimir, from the safety of his high beam.

'Help them!' cried Isam, leaping bravely into the midst of the terrified cats.

A few struck out at the blood-hound, which dropped the kitten and began biting his assailants. The cats retreated, some crying with pain, while the big dog advanced, his jaws open, ready to crunch and tear.

'So much for emperors,' murmured Delilah.

Casimir gave her a shifty glance. 'What would you do, then, clever sister?' he snapped.

'You don't know, do you?' said Delilah. 'You really don't! You never learned about dogspells.'

'Of course I didn't,' sneered Casimir. 'Who needs dogspells? We need an army. We need . . .'

'Be quiet and watch!' commanded Delilah. 'You need a dogspell right now, or you're going to lose half your troops!'

8

The Thief

Something in Delilah's tone must have reached the cats below. They all stopped howling and gazed up at her. Even the dog was distracted for a moment, and this gave Delilah just enough time to gather her strength.

She stared down at the dog's gloomy, wrinkled face. And he stared back, mesmerized, for Delilah was now glowing.

The doomed dog trembled as a shower of blazing stars fell from the shining coat and covered his muzzle. They sprinkled his back and his tail. His legs gave way and he began to shrivel.

'Bruiser! Where the devil are you?' a voice shouted.

But the dogspell could not be stopped. The cats drew back from the incredible shrinking dog as he twinkled and flickered. He looked like a very pretty Christmas tree, whose lights were slowly dying and whose needles were

57

withering. Not until the dog was smaller than the smallest kitten, did Delilah decide to release her victim. She watched him run out of the warehouse with his tiny tail tucked between his legs, and she smiled with satisfaction.

'What the . . .?' yelled the dog's master, dropping his torch. 'Who the . . .?' He slammed the doors shut and snapped the padlock with shaking hands. He was yelling with fright as he stumbled along the wet quay, desperate to get away.

The cats, breathless with admiration, raised their heads to Delilah and gave a loud cheer. Delilah graciously inclined her head. She could feel Casimir stiffen beside her, not pleased by Delilah's instant popularity.

'Perhaps, brother,' she said, 'you will now admit that you need me.'

'I can't say that I'm not impressed,' Casimir allowed, 'but still . . .'

'Well done! Brilliant! Fantastic! Marvellous, sister!' These compliments came from Isam who was speeding up a ladder. When he got to the top he ran along the balcony towards his brother and sister. 'Heroine!' he panted when he reached Delilah. 'Many could have died but for you!'

'Thank you, Isam,' she said.

'She will be such an asset, don't you agree, Casimir?' Isam said eagerly.

'I suppose . . .' muttered Casimir.

'Take your time,' Delilah turned her head away. 'It must be difficult to admit that your sister is something of a genius.'

'Casimir likes to think that only he can save us all,' declared the genial Isam. 'Don't take any notice of him. You *must* stay, Delilah. Say she must, Casimir!'

'You must stay, Delilah,' muttered Casimir.

'I'd be glad to,' replied Delilah, equally off-hand.

'Wonderful!' purred Isam.

The other cats were listening to their leaders' conversation with interest. They were all of the opinion that their lives would be a great deal easier if Delilah were there to protect them. They purred their approval when they heard her agree to stay.

'It's settled then,' said Casimir. 'But right now the fishing boats are coming in. It's time for breakfast.'

At these words the cats below began to swarm up the ladder.

'Wait, Casimir,' said Delilah. 'Can I take breakfast to our sister, Sorayah?'

'Sorayah's dead,' said Casimir. 'Do not speak of her.'

'But I found her,' cried Delilah, 'and helped her to escape.'

'Enough,' commanded Casimir. 'I won't listen to your stories. Now follow me,' and he

leapt for the hole in the roof.

Delilah did as she was told, and Isam scrambled after her. As soon as he was out, Casimir jumped on to the cliff. Delilah followed and down they flew, their paws sliding on the crumbling sandstone. And now Delilah could see the lights of the fishing boats, bouncing on the dark sea. One of the boats had already moored.

'We have a method,' Isam panted in Delilah's ear as they raced along the quay. 'I'd better explain.'

'We don't all rush at once. We form groups.

Six to a boat, but only two fetch.'

'Fetch?' inquired Delilah.

'Grab the fish,' explained Isam. 'To send more than two would annoy the fishermen. But they accept a few because we keep the rats down. Fishermen can't abide rats.'

'Tell me more,' said Delilah.

So Isam told Delilah how a group of cats would hide behind a warehouse while two approached the boat and brought back a fish each. These would be eaten by the group while the fetchers went back for two more. Of these one would be eaten by the fetchers, the other shared between four. The third fetching was the last, and the last two fish were carried back to the kittens and the wounded, who could not hunt for themselves.

'Very fair,' observed Delilah. 'But how do the fetchers get the fish?'

'One or two are always dropped, or slip out of the net,' Isam told her. Even as he spoke groups had formed and two fetchers were approaching the first boat. Delilah watched them from the shadows of a warehouse. Everything went according to plan. She was astonished by the small army's meticulous timing and most impressed by the way each group shared their fish so amicably. Soon, the first group had eaten their breakfast and were on the way back to the warehouse with two fish for the kittens. Delilah and Isam were in the last group to receive their breakfast. They were not fetchers, but tomorrow, Isam assured Delilah, she would be allowed to practise carrying.

'Couldn't I practise today, brother?' asked Delilah, thinking of Sorayah. 'If you can't trust me to fetch, surely I could carry a fish back to the kittens?'

Isam looked dubious.

'Please,' begged Delilah.

'Novices cannot begin until their second day; it's a rule,' argued Isam. 'Casimir doesn't like rules to be broken.'

'Casimir won't know until it's too late,' Delilah pointed out. 'He's already on his way back.'

'Very well,' Isam reluctantly agreed.

It was only when they began to ascend the cliff path that Delilah stopped and said, through a mouth full of fish, 'This fish is for someone else.'

Isam turned his head and stared back at her. 'What d'you mean?' he whispered.

'I mean that this fish is for our sister, Sorayah!'

'You mustn't say such things,' said Isam

sadly. 'I know that Sorayah is dead.'

'Not true, but she will be if she doesn't get this fish.'

'You're lying, Delilah,' Isam said angrily. 'We saw our sister lying stiff in a cage.'

'What's the trouble?' called Casimir. He always waited on the roof until every cat was safe inside the warehouse.

'It seems that our sister has other plans for the fish,' said Isam. 'She says it is for Sorayah!'

'Delilah wants the fish for herself,' growled Casimir.

Delilah didn't wait to hear any more. She bounded down the cliff and raced along the quay, with her angry brothers shouting behind her. 'Thief!' they shrieked as their feet pounded on the quay. They were stronger than she was and their legs were longer. Soon they would be on her. The only way she could convince them that Sorayah was alive was to lead them to her. But what if Sorayah had gone? Casimir and Isam would never trust Delilah again.

9

Dogspells

Sorayah woke up in a cold, damp place that she didn't recognize. She seemed to be caught in the well of a great bale of rope. The sky was a deep brilliant blue and seagulls were screaming over her. Beyond the birds' screeching she could hear shouting and the noise of winches, crates and breaking ice.

Sorayah huddled deeper into her hiding place. She felt too weak to escape. Her head swam, her tongue was dry and swollen and every limb ached. Where was her sister? She had promised to bring her a meal. She was dying of starvation. 'Oh, no,' Sorayah whimpered. 'I'm too young. I did so want to have kittens.'

She gazed longingly at the blue sky, perhaps for the last time. And then there was a scream and the shining silver moon fell out of the sky. As it dropped beside Sorayah, a voice full of pain called, 'I've brought you a fish, Sorayah. Eat it, quickly.'

A fish! The very smell of it cleared Sorayah's head. The touch of it on her tongue spread through her body like a flame. She began to devour the fish in great, gulping mouthfuls, unaware of the two heads peering down at her, until a voice said, 'So it's true!' And Sorayah looked up at two pairs of golden eyes.

'Isam! Casimir!' she cried. 'I thought I was doomed. Did you bring me the fish?'

'No,' Casimir said sheepishly.

'It wasn't us, sister,' Isam confessed. 'It was Delilah!'

'Delilah . . .' Sorayah struggled upright and peered over the edge of the rope.

Delilah sat in an angry huddle a few feet from the coiled rope. Her brothers had been very rough when they tried to get the fish away from her. Her nose was bloody and tufts of her fine grey hair lay all around her on the wet quay.

'What has happened to Delilah?' exclaimed Sorayah.

'We didn't believe . . .' Isam began.

'She broke the rules,' said Casimir.

'You *attacked* her,' Sorayah accused her brothers.

'Rules cannot be broken,' insisted Casimir.

'What rules?' Sorayah demanded, hauling

herself to the top of the rope. Already she felt better.

'We'll explain,' said Casimir. 'It's good to see you, sister. We thought you were . . . well, to be honest we thought you hadn't a chance.'

Delilah came cautiously towards them, and Isam said, 'Forgive us, Delilah. We have a code, and it must be honoured.'

'Delilah saved my life,' snapped Sorayah. 'Not once, but twice!'

'We didn't know,' said Casimir.

'We didn't believe, that's the truth,' admitted Isam. 'Forgive us, Delilah.'

'I forgive you,' she said haughtily, '*this* time.'

'What a team we shall be,' Casimir declared.

'The four of us, together again. How proud our mother Almira would be if she could see us now.'

'Not so proud if she could see her daughters!' Delilah wiped her bloody nose.

'We shall go back to the warehouse and "repair" ourselves,' suggested Isam.

As the four big cats walked back along the quay, sparkling dawn light spread across the sea, and the fishermen paused in their work to watch them. Sorayah's coat was not all that it should have been, and Delilah did not look her best, but even so the family was a magnificent and unusual sight.

By the time the four cats reached the warehouse, Sorayah was too exhausted to make the climb up to the roof. She rested in a small hollow at the bottom of the cliff and Delilah stayed with her, to keep her safe.

'Soon I shall teach you to make dogspells,' she told her sister. 'And I shall teach my brothers too, if they behave themselves. I am sure that Mustapha Marzavan bestowed the gift on all of us, but practice makes perfect.'

By the following night Sorayah felt strong enough to climb the cliff and jump through the hole in the warehouse roof. Casimir and Isam had told the other cats about their sister's great ordeal in the loathsome pet shop, and when she arrived on the high beam they all cheered heartily. Sorayah was moved to tears.

'Thank you! Thank you! But I wouldn't be here if it weren't for my brave sister Delilah.'

Whereupon they cheered Delilah even louder. Delilah acknowledged their applause, and then raising a paw for silence, she said 'When Sorayah is fully recovered my family and I are going to practise dogspells. It is a gift bestowed on us by Mustapha Marzavan, Breeder of Rare Cats. You are all welcome to come and watch.'

In a few days Sorayah had put on several pounds, thanks to the daily intake of fresh fish, and her fur and whiskers were once more thick and lustrous. It was time to find out if she and her brothers could rediscover their talent for dogspells. They set off after breakfast the following day. The four grey cats were followed by every able-bodied cat and kitten. They chose dogs unaccompanied by humans and they worked in secluded places: parks, gardens, empty beaches and deserted alleys. But the four big cats made such a striking group people couldn't help noticing them. Someone took a photograph of the cats, as they raced round an ornamental pond.

It didn't take Delilah's sister and brothers long to discover their talents. They smouldered and sparkled behind walls and fences, in shadowy trees and empty porches, while dogs whimpered and shivered and shrank. Casimir, always inclined to overdo things, wasn't content with shrinking one or two dogs, he had to shrink ten before he was satisfied with his performance.

It had already been agreed that they should

return the dogs to their original size after each experiment, but on one occasion Casimir was so delighted with his achievement he couldn't bear to bring an aggressive boxer back to shape. And then, quite by accident, he discovered another talent. He turned the dog into a bat.

The indignant dog-bat flew into Casimir's long fur, giving him the fright of his life.

'That will teach you to break *my* rules,' said Delilah, obligingly changing the bat into its former muscular dog shape. Unfortunately she forgot to disentangle the dog from Casimir's coat. It would be hard to say which was the most alarmed, the dog or Casimir. But after a wild tussle, the dog fled in a cloud of grey fur.

'I think we have had enough of dogspells for today,' said the embarrassed Casimir.

Every cat agreed with this and the performers and their audience went back to the warehouse, feeling pleasantly exhausted. They travelled in groups of four, so that they wouldn't attract too

much attention, but *someone* was watching them. Someone who was determined to get the army of cats out of his warehouse.

If the man who imprisoned the cats was evil, Guto Morgan was worse. He was a thief, who kept stolen goods hidden in rolls of plastic in the warehouse. The fishermen had often wondered what Guto Morgan was up to. He said that he kept carpets in his warehouse. But why did Guto only fetch and deliver them at night? His battered van was seldom seen in daylight.

They knew all about the cats living in Guto's warehouse and thought it was a great joke. 'The cats must know what he's hiding,' they told each other. But Guto had had enough of those cats. They were attracting too much attention. He suspected that the four big grey creatures had eaten his precious Bruiser. They looked rather valuable. Very soon the police would come snooping round, thinking he'd stolen them. Somehow Guto would have to get rid of them.

That night, as the cats were settling down to sleep, Sorayah noticed that her sister seemed wistful, even sad. Delilah had appeared to be such a cheerful, resilient character, Sorayah wondered what could be troubling her. She went and crouched close to Delilah. 'What is it, sister? What were you dreaming about? You look quite melancholy.'

'It's nothing,' Delilah declared. 'I was just thinking about my red velvet cushion with the gold braid and shiny tassles. It was so comfortable.'

'Was this in your old home?'

'It was.'

'Tell me about it,' begged Sorayah.

'There's not much to tell,' Delilah said coldly. 'For two winters and two summers I lived with a family called Pugh. Edward, the boy, looked after me. He made me believe that I was very precious to him, but then he deserted me, just like that! So much for human loyalty.'

'I can't believe he deserted you on purpose,' said Sorayah. 'Not after two winters and two summers.'

'Well, he did,' Delilah told her curtly.

'Are you sure?' persisted Sorayah. 'Boys who keep cats are not usually so thoughtless.'

'Hmph!' Delilah retorted. Refusing to discuss her past any more, she closed her eyes and pretended to be asleep. But before she drifted into her dreams she remembered the games she and Edward played, the toys he had bought her, the good food, the care and attention he had lavished on her. And then she thought of Tudor, her foster son, and felt a little twinge of guilt at leaving him so abruptly. She had been truly fond of Tudor. Well, that's all over now, Delilah told herself. Better forget them and think of the future.

After such an exciting day the cats were soon sleeping soundly. All except Casimir. The dog-bat incident had unsettled him. He was afraid to go to sleep in case he had nightmares about it. And in this fitful state Casimir heard a strange sound outside the warehouse: soft footfalls, a tinny sort of banging, a thump and then a quiet and sinister giggle. Had Isam heard these sounds he would have known that they meant danger.

10

Mr Fudge Moves in

When Edward got back from his holiday he looked for Delilah everywhere. He went next-door to see Annie, and he was surprised to find her hobbling about on crutches with a huge white plaster cast on her left leg. Annie told him all about her accident with the kite. 'And who fed Delilah while you were in hospital?' Edward asked.

Annie admitted that her parents had missed a couple of meals. 'But she's been eating regularly ever since I came home,' Annie told him.

'I hope she wasn't too upset,' Edward said. 'Does she look well?'

'I haven't actually seen her,' Annie confessed.

'What?' cried Edward.

'I thought she was sulking. Tudor's been acting rather strange, as a matter of fact.'

'In what way "strange"?' asked Edward, every moment becoming more alarmed.

'He keeps running off,' Annie told him, 'and

sometimes he won't eat. I think Delilah's hurt his feelings, she never comes to see him any more, and then there's that horrible cat . . .'

'What horrible cat?'

'The muddy-coloured thing that sits on your wall all day.'

Edward had noticed an odd-looking cat on the garden wall, but he hadn't paid it much attention, he'd been so eager to find Delilah.

'Something awful's happened,' he declared. 'I know it. Delilah's gone. Why didn't you realize? That strange cat has been eating her meals. How could you be so stupid, Annie?'

Annie was indignant. 'My leg hurts,' she cried. 'It's all I can think about. You know I'm in the netball team. I won't be able to play for ages next term.' Annie slammed the door in Edward's face.

Edward went home feeling angry and distressed. He searched for Delilah all evening, running up and down the street, calling in all the gardens, knocking on the neighbours' doors. But no one had seen the big grey cat.

It was almost dark when he got home. The strange cat jumped off the wall and rubbed itself against Edward's leg as he went through the gate.

'Get off!' he cried. 'Go away! You're not my cat!'

'Not yet,' said the cat with a sinister sort of purr.

Edward couldn't eat his supper. 'It's all your fault,' he shouted at his parents. 'You made me leave Delilah behind.'

'It wasn't us,' argued his father. 'It's the law. You can't take cats abroad, just like that. They have to go into quarantine for ages afterwards.'

'I didn't want to go abroad, did I?' Edward wailed, and he stomped off to his room, ready for a good long cry.

For three days Edward wouldn't speak to Annie. He wouldn't brush his hair, or change his socks or clean his teeth. 'What's the point?' he would mumble dismally. He wouldn't even touch the treats his mother tempted him with – crinkly chips, choc-chip ice-cream, jumbo sausages and cheesy toast. They were Delilah's favourites too.

'Edward lived for that cat,' Mrs Pugh told her husband with a sigh. 'I don't know what we're going to do!'

'Perhaps he'll take to the stray that always sits on our wall,' said Mr Pugh. 'Seems a nice enough little thing.' But he put an advertisement in the local paper, just in case. He described Delilah and asked for information. But no one called. Mrs Pugh contacted the Cats' Protection League, the vet and the RSPCA. None of them had seen Delilah.

Annie tried not to let Edward's mood depress her, but it wasn't easy, with her leg still in plaster and Tudor behaving so strangely. He had been sunk in gloom ever since Delilah disappeared. He missed her terribly, and the horrible Mr Fudge made things worse by taunting him and telling him that soon, he, Mr Fudge, would be living with the Pughs and enjoying all the perks that Delilah had enjoyed. 'She'll never come back,' Mr Fudge would snigger. 'Never! Never! Never!'

Tudor went on long, lonely walks, often staying out all night. Sometimes he would share a bed with his friend Tabby-Jack at the fabric shop, or he would visit the Orange Bomber, a champion fighter, always ready to help a lost cause. But neither of them had seen Delilah. 'If she's gone of her own accord, there's not much we can do,' said Tabby Jack.

'It's all the fault of that horrible Mr Fudge,' moaned Tudor. 'And now he's trying to take Delilah's place.'

Whenever Edward came into the garden, Mr Fudge would wind himself round the boy's legs, purring sweet nothings in an oily voice. It was very flattering. Edward couldn't help giving Mr Fudge the odd stroke, and then he started to feed him. One day, to Tudor's horror, Edward carried Mr Fudge indoors.

'That does it!' said Tudor. 'I'm off!' He ran home and slipped through his cat-flap, preparing to have a good meal before his journey. But he found Annie looking really

80

cheerful for once. She was waving a magazine about and shouting, 'I've found Delilah! I've found her!'

She hobbled over to the Pughs' house, still waving the magazine. Tudor followed her. For the first time since Delilah went, he began to feel hopeful.

'Edward!' Annie cried, banging on the Pughs' door. 'I've found her.'

Edward opened the door. 'What? Where?' he yelled.

'In *Paws* magazine. Look, there's a picture. I'm sure it's her.'

Edward led Annie into the kitchen and made her spread the magazine on the breakfast table. Toast and marmalade went flying.

'Really Edward,' grumbled Mrs Pugh, who

liked things tidy. But Edward looked so happy, she let the matter rest.

Tudor had followed Annie into the kitchen. He noticed that Mr Fudge was eating bacon and egg in Delilah's favourite place under the counter. Tudor growled softly at him. 'You haven't won yet,' he said.

Mr Fudge spat at Tudor and nudged his breakfast further under the counter.

Edward was turning the pages of the magazine excitedly. 'Where? Where?' he shouted.

'There!' Annie's finger pounced on a rather misty photograph at the bottom of page five.

'How can you tell it's Delilah?' wailed Edward.

'Read!' commanded Annie. 'Read what it says.'

So Edward read aloud:

Four magnificent grey cats have recently been observed in Summersea, on the west coast. Even one of these cats on the loose would be an unusual sight, as they are obviously very valuable. But the fact that there are four is even more remarkable. Several people in the area have linked their appearance to the mysterious, albeit temporary, disappearance of dogs. Some of the dogs concerned behave in a very odd way when their owners find them. 'My Tinker went a bit mad,' said Mrs H. of Beehive Drive. 'He kept biting his tail, as if he wanted to make sure it was still there.'

'What d'you think?' asked Annie, watching Edward's face for a glimmer of hope.

'I think,' said Edward slowly, 'I think that you're a genius, Annie. And I think that one of those cats *must* be Delilah!'

'Because the dogs have shrunk?'

'Obviously.'

'But what about the other cats?'

Edward shrugged. 'It says that the photograph was sent in by the *Summersea Gazette*. I've got to get to Summersea as soon as possible.'

Mrs Pugh said, 'Not a chance this week, Edward. We're busy, your dad and I.'

Edward moaned.

'My dad'll take us,' said Annie. 'He's got a few days off. He asked me if I'd like a day out, but I couldn't think where I wanted to go.'

'Summersea?' asked Edward. 'Do you think . . .'

'Course,' said Annie. 'It's all my fault that Delilah went.'

Edward and Annie rushed off to see Mr Watkin as fast as Annie's leg would allow. But Tudor lingered for a moment in the Pughs' kitchen. Soundlessly he approached Mr Fudge, then crouching very close to the ugly cat he hissed, 'Something tells me your days are numbered!'

Mr Fudge screamed, 'Go to hell!'

Mrs Pugh dropped a frying-pan and shouted, 'Get out, both of you!'

Mr Watkin happily agreed to take Annie and Edward to Summersea. 'But it's a long journey,' he said, 'so we'd better set off early.'

'With the dawn chorus?' asked Annie, who knew her father had been up very early just lately, recording bird song.

'A bit later than that,' said Mr Watkin. 'Six o'clock suit you?'

'Yes,' Annie and Edward agreed.

'The sooner the better,' said Edward. 'Someone might see the photo and try and claim Delilah. *Paws* is a very popular magazine.'

It was even more popular than Edward imagined. *Paws* was read in every corner of the globe. And two very unusual cat-lovers had already embarked on a long journey to rescue the four grey cats.

That night Edward lay in bed thinking of all the things he would tell Delilah when he found her. He would never leave her again. But first he would have to find her, and that might not be easy.

It did not occur to Edward that Delilah might not want to come home.

11

Poison – and Worse

Casimir was listening to the soft footsteps outside the warehouse. When the footsteps had receded he crept away from the sleeping cats and climbed up to his high beam. He was wide awake now and eager to know what had been going on outside. Should he tell Isam about the strange noises? No. His brother was fast asleep, it would be a shame to wake him. So the big cat climbed out on to the roof alone. When he was on the cliff path he could see a long trough, a gutter perhaps, outside the warehouse. It was full of food. Meat! Casimir raced towards it. 'Meat!' he purred. 'Such a nice change from fish!'

He reached the trough and gulped down a piece of meat, just as a voice cried, 'No, Casimir!'

Casimir looked up. But it was too late. A fiery pain shot through his body, and he sank to the ground. Through a blur of agony he saw

Delilah racing towards him; he thought he heard her shout 'Poison!' and then his world grew cold and silent.

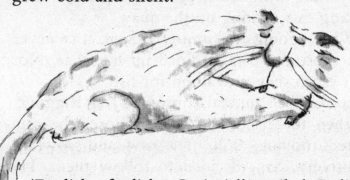

'Foolish, foolish, Casimir!' wailed Delilah, sniffing her brother's coat. She could smell the deadly poison racing through his body.

The other cats heard her and came running down the cliff. 'Get back!' screeched Delilah. 'Don't let the kittens out! There's poison everywhere.'

The other cats stopped, frozen by Delilah's imperious voice.

'Is Casimir . . . is he dead?' whispered Sorayah.

'No,' Delilah told her. 'I think I stopped him in time. But we must dilute the poison. We must get him to drink.'

Casimir began to moan.

'The fishermen. We'll get them to help,' Isam proposed. 'They'll soon be coming in.'

Skipper Sam Rogers and his mate, Jack Rigging, were the first fishermen on the scene. They were intrigued to see a row of mournful-looking cats waiting on the quay.

'What's going on?' muttered Sam. 'I've never seen those big cats all lined up like that. Not even when they're waiting for fish.'

'Looks like a funeral,' observed Jack Rigging.

When the fishermen were ashore, the cats started moving, still in a row and yowling plaintively. Sam decided to follow them. He found Casimir lying beside the trough of meat and immediately guessed what had happened. 'That Guto Morgan,' Sam muttered. 'He needs sorting. A villain, that's what he is. Wait till I get my hands on him.'

Sam rushed off to fetch the pint of milk he kept in the boat for his morning tea. 'Guto Morgan's poisoning cats now,' he shouted, 'the evil so-and-so! One of the cats looks pretty bad. We'll have to get rid of the stuff before any more of them eat it.'

Jack followed him back to the warehouse and while Sam tried to coax a little milk past Casimir's clenched teeth, Jack shovelled the poisoned meat into bags.

'We'll burn it,' said Jack. 'It's the only way.'

Casimir slowly regained consciousness. The

pain was still terrible but he had recovered from the shock; his vision was blurred and sounds were muffled, but he could hear a voice, Delilah's, he thought, urging him to drink. 'Drink! Drink! Drink!' Other voices joined in with Delilah.

Someone was supporting Casimir, a man with strong fish-smelling hands. Casimir tried to turn his head. The man helped him to reach a bowl of milk and Casimir drank. How thirsty he was. He thought he would never have enough of the cool delicious liquid.

'Drink! Drink! Drink!' chanted the voices.

Now Casimir could feel the liquid in his belly. It was good. And then, all at once, he wanted to be alone. To be private.

'Go away,' he mewed.

The other cats backed off. Sam let Casimir get to his feet and very shakily, the big tom dragged himself behind the warehouse, where he was violently sick. But he felt better, much better.

Casimir peered round the warehouse and mewed, 'Thanks!'

'I think your friend is going to be all right,' Sam told the other cats. 'Come on, Jack. We'd better get back to the fish.'

When the cats began to climb up to the warehouse roof, Casimir called feebly, 'No! It isn't safe here any more.'

'He's right,' said Isam. 'The evil one will be back. He won't give up until he's killed us all. You must leave here, every one of you. Hide in parks, in woods and in fields. And don't come back until it's safe.'

'How will we know when it's safe?' asked a sensible tabby cat.

'The fishermen will let you know,' Sorayah told her. 'They're our friends. They'll make sure you're all right.'

'We're going to stay here,' Delilah announced. 'We're going to make it safe for you to return.'

'How?' asked a bold Siamese.

'That's for us to know,' replied Delilah. 'Go on, now! Buzz off, all of you.'

The crowd of bemused cats began to creep uncertainly along the quay. Some of them picked up the fish that Sam and his friends threw in their direction. Others looked too confused to respond.

'Farewell, friends,' called Isam. 'We have taught you how to survive, and you can come back to the harbour soon. We'll never forget you, wherever we are.'

'Why did you say that?' Sorayah asked her brother. 'It sounded so – final.'

'I said it because I believe we have reached an ending, I sense that something extraordinary is about to occur; something that will change our lives forever.'

The others said nothing. They too had begun to feel a mysterious stirring in the air. Good? Evil? They were both there; one borne on the wind from the sea, the other from the dark cliff behind them. Casimir's legs were still shaky, so his family had to support him up the cliff path, and then help him to jump on to the roof. But the effort took all his strength and once inside the warehouse, he lay on the beam gasping for breath. Delilah, crouching beside him, felt close to despair. And then she began to tremble with rage. What was wrong with human beings? Some of them so easily gave in to wickedness.

If only she knew how to cast manspells. 'You know what we have to do, don't you?' she whispered.

'I am beginning to hear your thoughts, Delilah,' said Sorayah.

'Tell me,' said Isam.

'We have to make a manspell,' said Delilah.

'We can't!' exclaimed her brother. 'We have only been given one gift each, and that is for casting dogspells.'

'One gift each,' Delilah murmured. 'But there are four of us. Perhaps the strength of four can make a manspell.'

'It wouldn't be allowed,' Casimir remarked in a thin voice. 'Natural laws must not be broken.'

'Sometimes they have to be,' Delilah told him.

'Let's wait and see,' suggested Sorayah. 'Perhaps we won't have to use such drastic methods.'

The four cats closed their eyes and dozed for a while, gathering their strength for the day to come. A little after midday the fishermen went home and the harbour was deserted. A cold mist crept in from the sea. The boats creaked and whined at their moorings, and the screaming seagulls sounded apprehensive. The sun disappeared and an eerie darkness descended. It was then that Guto Morgan made his first move.

Delilah was the first to hear him, thumping over the roof; dragging, pulling, scraping. Before she could understand what was happening, the gap in the roof had been covered with a thick sheet of polythene. A rock was then dropped over it. More rocks followed. By now all the cats were awake.

'Can he be mending the roof?' muttered Casimir.

'Not mending,' Delilah said.

They began to relax in the long silence that followed. Perhaps Guto wasn't interested in them after all. And then it happened. The doors were flung open and a monster roared into the warehouse. A great truck, with lights blazing and a thundering, foul-smelling exhaust.

The cats tried to focus on the shadowy figure that leapt out of the cab, but they were blinded by the headlights. The warehouse doors slammed shut and they could hear Guto laughing as he hammered a board across the doors.

'There's no way out,' gasped Isam.

The truck roared on, and the warehouse began to fill with deadly, poisonous gas.

12

The Enemy

When the travellers reached Summersea, Mr Watkin decided to visit the local newspaper office first, to find out the address of the man who had taken the photo of the four big cats. But there was no one at home when they called on the photographer, so Mr Watkin suggested they have breakfast. They chose a bright café close to the harbour, and ordered bacon and eggs.

Edward couldn't eat. 'So far, no good,' he sighed.

'Now then, Edward, be positive,' said Mr Watkin, and he played a tune on the teacups to cheer the boy's spirits.

'The photo was taken near the park, so let's start there,' suggested Annie.

'Good thinking, Annie!' said Mr Watkin.

After breakfast Edward and Mr Watkin spent an hour searching the park while Annie sat on a bench. There seemed to be a great many cats hiding in the trees and shrubs, but none answered Edward's feeble call of 'Delilah!' Next Edward and Mr Watkin explored the roads leading to the harbour. Annie stayed in the car. Her good leg was beginning to ache. There was a cat in nearly every garden. But not the right cat. They tried the shops. Some of the shopkeepers had *heard* about the four grey cats and one of them had actually seen them. 'They were marching down Harbour Road,' she said, 'bold as brass. Great big grey cats. Never seen anything like them.'

'We've tried the Harbour Road,' said Edward gloomily.

'Have you tried the harbour, love?' asked the

woman. 'I've heard people say they live there. They like the fish, you see.'

'The harbour,' said Edward, looking more cheerful. 'Let's try it, Mr Watkin.'

Mr Watkin drove down to the harbour. 'I don't like the look of that mist,' he said.

Edward got out of the car and ran beside the water. He called Delilah's name over and over again. The mist rolled, thick and damp, around the fishing boats. Soon Edward could hardly see them. 'Delilah!' he called mournfully.

'I'm starving,' Annie told her father. 'Could we have lunch now?'

'Good idea,' said Mr Watkin.

They returned to the café where Mr Watkin and Annie had eaten such a good breakfast.

'Perhaps the mist will lift this afternoon,' said Mr Watkin.

Edward managed to drink a Coke, but he still looked dreadful. His damp hair fell over his eyes and his cheeks were streaked with dirt. His tee-shirt was crumpled and stained and his jeans were muddy. Annie was shocked. Edward looked nothing like the smart boy who had moved into the house next door nearly two years ago. Delilah had almost broken Edward's

heart, Annie decided. Whatever was going to become of him if they didn't find her?

Edward was watching the misty harbour. He never took his eyes off it. A large truck rolled past the café and on down towards the water.

The exhaust was belching plumes of black smoke.

'Look at that,' said Mr Watkin. 'It's a disgrace. Polluting the air. It should be banned from the road.'

'Can we go back to the harbour?' Edward suddenly stood up. 'Now!'

'Not till I've finished my doughnut,' said Annie.

'But I've got a feeling,' said Edward, 'a feeling of doom!'

'Now then! Now then!' Mr Watkin hummed a tune while Annie licked her fingers.

Edward was in despair. 'I'm going now,' he cried. 'I can't wait!' He rushed out of the café and disappeared into the mist before they could stop him.

'Silly boy,' said Mr Watkin. He paid the bill as quickly as he could while Annie made herself comfortable on her crutches.

They couldn't see Edward anywhere, but they found a fisherman scrubbing the counters in one of the warehouses. He happened to be Sam Rogers' older brother Jim. 'I've seen a boy,' he said, 'went past a few minutes after that truck. It was off down to Guto Morgan's place.'

'Guto Morgan's place?' Mr Watkin inquired.

'It's right at the end of the harbour,' Jim said,

'under the cliff.'

Annie and her father began to walk towards the cliff, though they could hardly see it. Mist swirled across the quay, a thick broth of salt and seaweed. But lingering in the sea smells, Annie thought she could detect something else, something – almost exotic. Then, from the end of the harbour, they heard Edward shouting, and the muffled roar of an engine.

Mr Watkin ran while Annie hobbled behind him. He found Edward tugging at the doors of a battered-looking warehouse. From behind the doors came the deafening sound of an engine.

'Delilah's in there,' yelled Edward. 'I called

and she answered.'

'Are you sure?' said Mr Watkin, who could hear nothing beyond the noise of the truck.

'Of course!' bawled Edward. 'They're all in there. All four cats. I heard them crying. But now they're quiet. Someone's trying to kill them with carbon monoxide.'

'I can't believe it.'

'Believe it!' shouted Edward. 'Oh, Mr Watkin, please help. Quickly! We must open the doors or the cats will die.'

Annie arrived, huffing and puffing. 'Do something, Dad!' she cried.

Jim Rogers came running up to find out what all the commotion was about. 'The old devil,' he said. 'I knew he was up to no good. The boy's right. Guto failed to poison those cats this morning. Now this.'

'Please *do* something,' begged Edward.

'Hang on,' said Jim, already running back to the boats. He returned with a bundle of tools and began to attack the doors with a crowbar. The plank came away quite easily, but the padlock and chain were another matter.

Edward picked up a rock and tried to smash the chain.

'It'll need a hacksaw,' said Jim Rogers.

Edward beat on the door with his rock, over

and over again, bruising his fingers and tearing his tee-shirt.

'Steady, boy,' said Mr Watkin anxiously. 'It's a big building. It'll take a while to affect the cats.'

The truck engine roared on, its deadly fumes filling every corner of the warehouse. Jim began to saw the chain and slowly the metal gave way. The chain was almost broken when a huge man loomed up behind the group. 'What d'you think you're doing?' he bellowed. 'That's private property.'

'You've left an engine on in an enclosed place, and that's against the law,' said Jim.

'It's my business!' roared Guto, raising a fist.

'Now get away from that door!'

Jim backed away.

'But Mr – er – Morgan,' began Mr Watkin, who was a very tall man but not nearly as wide as Guto. Suddenly he didn't feel like arguing. That's when Annie swung out one of her crutches and brought it back THWACK! behind Guto's knees.

The big man gave a howl of pain and Annie shouted, 'Quick, Edward!' Edward leapt to the doors and tugged at the almost severed chain, while Jim and Mr Watkin took courage and held on to Guto. All at once the chain fell off and Edward pulled the big doors open. A deathly stench drifted out of the warehouse. Everyone started coughing and choking but Edward, pulling his tee-shirt over his nose and mouth, dashed into the dark warehouse.

'No, Edward,' spluttered Mr Watkin as Guto

broke free and pursued the boy.

Edward wrenched open the cab door and jumped inside. He turned the ignition key and the engine shuddered and died. After such thunder, the sudden silence was awesome.

'Get out of there, boy!' Guto held the open door. His face was purple with rage.

Edward stared at Guto. He suddenly felt sick and dizzy.

'Get out, I say!' roared Guto.

Edward froze. He shut his eyes tight, waiting for Guto's fist. But nothing happened. When Edward ventured a quick peep at Guto, something was happening to the big man. His mouth hung open, and he was staring into the air. Slowly Guto began to sink. But he wasn't just subsiding, he was getting smaller and smaller.

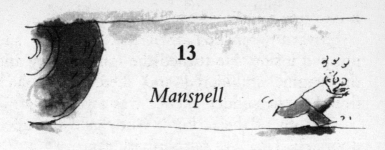

13

Manspell

Edward looked through the windscreen and there, glittering on a high beam, he made out four huge shapes. Their long wild fur seemed to be scattered with burning stars. Their upright tails were threaded with blazing colour, and their eyes were so golden-bright they were almost too painful to look at. Edward held his breath as Guto Morgan dwindled and shrivelled, and his loud voice faded to a muffled squeak. The cats were relentless. Still their victim withered. Smaller and smaller. Now he was out of sight, below the level of the cab floor. Edward couldn't bring himself to lean out of the truck and discover what had become of the villain, so he never saw a tiny mouse-sized man scuttle out of the warehouse before turning to dust.

Jim and Mr Watkin and Annie didn't see him either. They were gazing at the sparkling cats. The two men couldn't believe their eyes.

'Whatever is it?' whispered Jim. 'Phosphorescence?'

'Mmmmmm!' hummed Mr Watkin.

'It's a dogspell,' Annie said in a hushed voice. 'Only this time it's a manspell.'

'Manspell? What's that?' Jim asked nervously.

Mr Watkin frowned at Annie and hummed again.

Gradually the astonishing display began to wane.

'Did you see?' cried Edward rushing out.

'Yes,' said Annie breathlessly. 'We did, didn't we, Dad?'

Mr Watkin nodded slowly, and Jim whistled through his teeth. Now they could see that the warehouse was littered with torn polythene. The desperate cats had ripped the plastic rolls apart, spilling the contents: televisions, computers, candlesticks, clocks and silver bowls lay in untidy heaps all over the floor.

'What a haul,' Jim declared. 'I knew that Guto was a villain. Where is he now?'

'Gone,' said Edward. 'Gone forever!'

'Bless me!' Jim gulped. 'I never . . .'

He was cut short by the appearance of four majestic grey cats. They walked out of the gloom at the back of the warehouse, with their heads raised and tails like upright plumes. They looked neither to the left, nor to the right. In fact they seemed completely unaware of the four humans; their golden eyes were focused on a bright haze that surged along the quay.

The children and the two men drew back as the cats passed. They all felt that something remarkable was happening. Later, Annie would say that it was like having your skull frozen for a while. As the humans gazed at the cats, two forms emerged from the mist. They wore long coloured robes and their wrists and fingers glittered with jewels. The tallest of the two beckoned the cats. He spoke in a foreign language and his voice had a deep musical chime.

'Mustapha Marzavan,' breathed Isam. 'We are safe.'

'He has come to take us home,' said Casimir.

'Back across the water,' sighed Sorayah.

As the four cats approached the two robed figures, someone sang out, 'Delilah!'

It was Mustapha Marzavan's youngest

daughter. How Delilah had longed to hear her again. But the sound became strangely muddled in her head. It had a different tone, now. It was a boy's voice, loud and desperate.

Delilah stopped and looked over her shoulder. She saw Edward, his hair on end, his face streaked with dirt and tears. What a mess he looked. 'Forgive me, Delilah,' he sobbed.

'Don't look back, Delilah!' called Sorayah. 'Come, quickly!'

But Delilah did not move.

'Delilah,' cried her brothers. 'Come!'

'Edward needs me,' she said softly.

'Are you mad, sister?' said Sorayah. 'He deserted you.'

'I think,' murmured Delilah, 'that he deserves a second chance.'

'No, no, no!' Sorayah was beside herself. 'We'll never see you again.'

'I shall think of you often,' Delilah told her, 'safe in Mustapha Marzavan's great cat-parlour. Farewell, sister!'

'You did your best, Edward,' Annie said. 'You saved Delilah's life. Think of it like that.'

'But I want her back,' Edward whispered.

The robed figures had turned away. Beyond them a strange craft could just be glimpsed; a boat with a wide grey hull. The strangers stepped aboard and the cats followed, one by one. And then a dense swirl of mist shrouded them all, and the distant throb of a motor could be heard. When the mist lifted, the boat had gone and the quay was deserted. Except for one grey cat, standing alone and gazing out to sea. Slowly she turned and came walking back to Edward.

'Delilah!' Edward sighed, and a big smile spread across his grubby face.